To Lonelyville

Copyright © 2014 by Tad Hills
All rights reserved. Published in the United States by
Schwartz & Wade Books, an imprint of Random House
Children's Books, a division of Random House LLC,
a Penguin Random House Company, New York.
Schwartz & Wade Books and the colophon are trademarks
of Random House LLC.
Visit us on the Web! randomhouse.com/kids
Educators and librarians, for a variety of teaching tools,
visit us at RHTeachersLibrarians.com

Library of Congress Cataloging-in-Publication Data
Hills, Tad. Duck & Goose go to the beach /written and
illustrated by Tad Hills.   pages cm
Summary: "Duck wants to go on an adventure. Goose doesn't. He
doesn't see the point. After all, why would they go anywhere when
they're happy right where they are? But then Goose sees the ocean
and loves it. Who doesn't? Well, Duck, for one" —Provided by publisher.
ISBN 978-0-385-37235-0 (hardback) — ISBN 978-0-385-37237-4 (glb)
—ISBN 978-0-385-37236-7 (ebook)
[1. Ducks—Fiction. 2. Geese—Fiction. 3. Adventure and adventurers—
Fiction. 4. Beaches—Fiction. 5. Friendship—Fiction.] I. Title. II. Title:
Duck and Goose go to the beach.
PZ7.H563737Duan 2014   [E]—dc23   2013029728

The text of this book is set in Bodoni Old Face.
The illustrations were rendered in oil paint.
MANUFACTURED IN CHINA
10 9 8 7 6 5 4 3 2 1
First Edition

Duck & Goose
Go to the Beach

written & illustrated by Tad Hills

schwartz & wade books · new york

"Don't you just love it here, Duck?" Goose honked.

The two friends relaxed in the early-morning sun and listened to the hum of the meadow. Butterflies flitted and grass swished in the breeze.

"Yes, I do," Duck agreed.

"Let's never leave," said Goose.

Suddenly, Duck jumped up. "You just gave me the greatest idea, Goose!" he quacked. "Let's leave! Let's go away!"

"A-*WHAT?!*" Goose honked.

"A-*WAY*. Let's take a trip."

Goose gulped. "A TRIP? A trip sounds far away. I like *close*."

"We could go on an adventure!" Duck said.

"An adventure? That sounds scary," Goose honked.

"Come on, Goose. A hike might be fun," Duck quacked.

"A hike?" said Goose. "That sounds like a fine way to twist your ankle."

Duck sighed. He gazed across the meadow toward a distant hill and began walking.

Goose followed. "I will walk, but I will not hike," he grumbled.

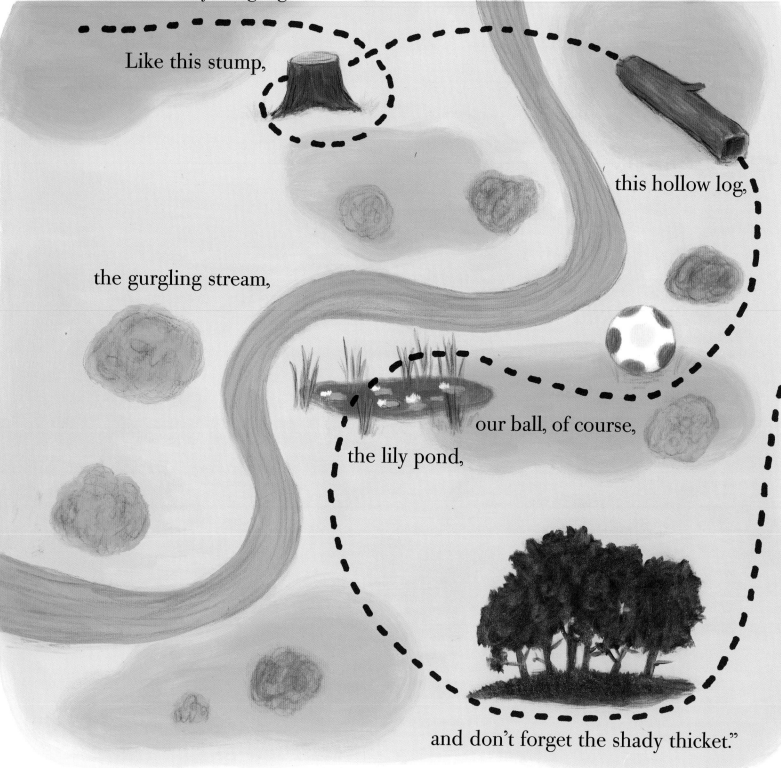

"Why would anyone want to leave this meadow?" Goose wondered aloud. "It has everything right here.

Like this stump,

this hollow log,

the gurgling stream,

our ball, of course,

the lily pond,

and don't forget the shady thicket."

Duck and Goose floated along a
stream they'd never floated along before.

They walked by a
pile of stones they'd
never walked by before

and passed the biggest
tree they'd ever seen.

They walked across fields
and up and down hills.

By the time Goose reached
the top of the highest hill, Duck
was already gazing off into
the distance.

"What's that?" he quacked.

"Could it be the beach?" Goose honked.

Duck's tail twitched with excitement. "I'm pretty sure I love the beach!"

"You've been to the beach?" asked Goose.

"No, not yet," said Duck, and he took off down the hill.

"Follow me, Goose! We are going to the beach!"

Goose chased after Duck.
"But, Duck, we already had our adventure," he called.

"Wait!" he shouted.

"Slow down!" he honked.

But Duck did not slow down.

Goose followed him through the brambles and tall grass until, finally, Duck stopped.

"I think we have arrived at the beach," said Duck.

"Oh my, the beach is LOUD!" yelled
Duck over the sound of the waves. "I can
barely hear my own quack."

Goose stared at the vast stretch of sky,
sand, and sea. "Isn't it magnificent?" he said.

"Oh dear, the beach has SO MUCH water," quacked
Duck. "I feel tiny."

"Have you ever seen SO MUCH sand?" honked Goose.

"It's getting in my feathers, and it's too hot on my feet,"
said Duck. "Let's go."

"Go swimming? Good idea, Duck!" said Goose, and
he raced to the water's edge.

"No, Goose! Wait for me!"

Duck dipped his hot feet in the water.
"Goose, you know these waves are very—"

"These waves are very FUN? Is that what you
were going to say, Duck?" honked Goose.
"No, not exactly."

The two friends strolled along the beach. They met the locals.

Some were friendly.

Others were not.

Some were shy.

Others were not.

Goose thought Duck might enjoy searching for
sea creatures under the rocks and seaweed.
He did not.

"Be careful, Goose.
You don't know what's
in there," Duck quacked.

They built a drip castle.

And they listened to the gentle roar of the ocean from deep within a seashell. It made Duck homesick.

"It sounds just like our gurgling stream," he quacked.

Later in the day, when the sand had cooled and the waves had settled, Duck and Goose relaxed.

"I like the smell of the beach," Goose said.

"Me too," Duck agreed. "But not as much as the meadow."

"Well, there's no place like the meadow," honked Goose.

"That's very true," said Duck.

So in the late afternoon, Duck and Goose followed their long shadows home.

They talked about their exciting day and about the friends they'd met. They talked about the hot sand and the cool water, the noisy crashing waves and the quiet tidal pools.

Back in the meadow at last, they watched the sun set.
Birds sang and grass swished in the breeze.

They both agreed that it was nice to be home.

"Duck, where should we go next?" Goose asked.

Duck closed his eyes. "How about to sleep?"